MY GRANDMA

RASHI SEN

ISBN 979-888521631-9

Contents

About

My grandma was born to a family of small village called Baghraji. Her name is kusum. When she and her four younger siblings were small their father passed away. Till the time her father was alive they were happy, sufficient, blessed with food to eat and clothes to wear. But after that they didn't have enough food for even one time.

My grandma had to quit her studies and look for a work to gain money for her family. That time she was in 4th class and about to go in 5th, she was so studious and intelligent among all her classmates but unfortunately she could not be able to continue

As the situation started getting normal after two years a situation of drought came to her life.

That time there was a scheme called Rahatkar where people used to go for work and get money but most of the time whether they get no money or sometimes not paid according to their work.

She and her mother used to go their from morning to late night but mostly return to home with no money in their hands. They sleep many nights with just a glass of water. It's very hard and heart breaking isn't it.

Witnessing her siblings crying and starving for food was obnoxious and like a night for her. For which she even begged for food from her neighbours. Constantly she was fighting for food, clothes and a

normal lifestyle for her family but nothing seemed to work out. The situation of drought was difficult for everyone at that time, there was no proper items available for daily needs.

After few years she got married, as her mother could not be able to afford all the expenses so her Mama helped in all expenses. After marriage her life started getting normal, she was happy and satisfied with all what she got. Her husband was well equipped to take care of her and also a loving husband. She delivered 8 children's in alternative years among which she had 2 miscarriage.

Those times ladies used to get scared of operation and any other treatments that's why they find ways to cure at home only. This results lack of hygiene and improper deliveries also unwanted miscarriages of ladies.

She was 45 year old when her husband passed due to cardiac arrest, the situation was unbearable and unbelievable for as she could have to lead her rest of life without her husband. There are so many responsibilities to fulfil, how she will going to do all?

She raised her four children with confidence ,care and love. There was nothing less in her parenting of her children. They all four got good jobs and life partners they wished for or even better. They never felt like they don't have a father in presence of their mother. It was not easy for her to manage all expenses and also to give good values to her children.

Despite of being illiterate she knows the value of education and work hard to provide proper education for them. Life of my grandma is inspiration for people who want to do something big in their life even having no facilities and guidance.

INTRODUCTION

Things will come to you and go. It's better to value them on time. Sometimes staying busy in our own deeds we fail to see the magic standing right infront of us. It doesn't mean being self-esteem is wrong but taking your loved ones as facetious does. Never allow your hauteur to take decisions and outlook of your life cause it is the biggest enemy of humankind. It is mentioned in Ramayana that "if relationships can be made through egoism than Sita will be called as beloved of Ravana not Ram."

Every flower has its own smell and beauty. Never depreciate someone on the basis of their appearance or outlook. May be you can't able to see the esoteric astounding

qualities of that person. Every flower takes its own time to blossom, to grow and to smell. We respect and let cherish them. God has given you life to learn things, make your name proud and to spread love among personage.

Learn new things everyday with immense joy and excitement. Never feel hesitation or any type of discomposure from learning new things in any age by any age teaching you.

"This life is like a treasure which we should keep chasing it by ignoring foolish norms and focusing only on our skills".

Almighty has offer you a wonderful and priceless life lets just thank him and make both God and your name proud. In this cosmos people take birth and die, one thing that stays even

after their death is their name and good works. Inner beauty is the most important thing to lead a happy life.

This body is mortal, we have no control over deaths and births, so lets focus on doing always good for needy and give respect to every creature that God has created.

I

MENTOR OF LIFE

In India, grandparents are personified as a Banyan tree , its stem as members of family and small buds as children or new members. Grandparents of house guides their family members with love, peace and most importantly their experience. Their experience helps very much for understanding the various aspects of life and how to deal with difficult situations. They are considered to be the first and proximate moral teacher of their children's and grandchildren's.

Many times situation occurs when you get confused or bewildered to take a step there your elders experience helps you a lot.

Sometimes bookish knowledge also fails

to show you right path then all you will need is someone's support and guidelines.

For our grandparents we are meant to be the whole world, they feel contentment to shower their love on us. Their love is so pure and unconditional. They don't want to see their grandchildren's in trouble or to face any kind of difficulty.

The delection they get when they help us in our problems or anything is priceless. We just have to keep faith in them and to avoid this erroneous norms that they know nothing, they can't be able to do that, they can't understand my situation.

Life is like a roller coaster full of ups and downs, happiness and sorrows, sometimes you feel alone and may be after a whi

accompanied etc are all parts of journey of life. People will come and go, teach you many things you don't know before. I want to include here an example of my life where my grandma's words proves to be as life changing words for our whole family

Everyone starts with a small and first step to achieve success in their life.

Similarly, my father did also by doing a job of small scale as lineman(to keep checks on wires of electricity in transformers and places and if something went wrong do repair it) in electricity department , a job that carries to much risk.

My grandma always used to ask my father that do your education complete because it is the only way to get higher possession and to be free from this risky works

He always used to ignore her advice and takes her

lightly by not giving attention. But nature has it's own way to teach you lesson, one day my father was doing his job as always under transformers.

Suddenly, wires of one transformer started burning and began to falls down on the ground. It was an unpredictable and dangerous accident that took place. Everyone starts getting panicking and screaming, unluckily my father was caught in that fire.

The people who were present there rush him to the hospital as soon as possible and the rest started to control the fire by calling fire Brigade. When my father reached hospital, doctors directly take him to the ICU and started doing all necessities,

doctor said that he is 78/ burnt and it will be very difficult to save him. It was the situation of life and death.

Our whole family was in shock and prayed continuously for my father, chanting God's name with a hope to him fine and healthy again. I still remember then I was just 8 year old and witnessing every single moment of that accident, people were coming and sympathizing us, faces of every family member , it was like a night mare.

Somewhere everyone just have a hope that God will do best. It was God's grace and obligation that after a few months he was able to walk , talk and able to do his work by own. He started a new life or new beginning, that accident taught him abundant of lesson he was

ignoring. My grandma had an conversation with him in which she told him that if would listen her earlier and completed his education this would never happened with him.

Then he realized that whatever she said was right and decided to complete his education. And today he is in good post and health by his efforts and believe. That was the day, when I comprehend that whatever our elders ask us to do or whenever they give us an advice regarding our stumbling block or entity always have a reason behind. The most far-reaching thing is they are experienced and know this world better than us.

"They know when to step in and when to step out".

We sometimes take decision not even thinking at once that what it will result and its consequences, whether it will be good for us or not. It's virtuous and ethical to listen our grandparents and follow their behest for our hunky- dory future.

II

MONEY A RESCUER

It's a say that "Save money today so that money can save you tomorrow", I totally agree with this, we as a human buys things just to impress and show off the society , even the things which are of no use we just buy it just to prove our superiority infront of them. Money and time are taken as compeer in all aspects, as both should be use wisely and avoid spending on unwanted things.

Money is considered to be as an elder brother of a person whenever we get in trouble or any kind of difficulty, money as an elder brother helps us to get free from our problems.

Learn the value of each penny, know the difference your spending money as a fool or master. You should have a command on money neither money have. Spend your money on things that have values or can come to your use, never get fooled with your need and fascination.

We must have noticed this a rich person have so many friends and relatives where as poor have minimal why?

Because people do friendships on the basis of your status, income, stardom and all. They always wants to attract you and spend time with you . They asserts to have so much care and love for you like a well wisher but when the day comes you have left with nothing with you than suddenly all these relatives and friends will turns into strangers. Choose your friends on the basis of what they want from you whether its you or your wealth, their love for you is real or just transitory.

Most of the people losses money because of their greediness , there are many offers and games that assure to get double amount like gambling, poker and many. You also cannot be able to realize this ever that they become your habit from hobby or amusement. For a momentary happiness don't let your money to be wasted in such things.

It has been said that investing money to buy food for your stomach and brain will give you boon for long run. So spend your money in getting healthy items for your body health to get a sound body and on your good education because

it' very important to be literate and well being. It will help you to get job and change your situation of getting troubles.

Things that can help you to save money and by which you can avoid your mistakes while s pending your money in stuffs are-

Before buying something just make sure it will be useful or not, don't buy unnecessary things.

Make a note of every penny spent, and see where your most of the money is spending and how you can control.

Save 20/ amount from your income or you can save more and get interest of that.

Never spend money on costly things to soon, wait for days and think

about it. If you think that you still want it then you can buy that.

Use alternative of things you want to buy for example, you can cook dishes on home and can avoid fancy restaurant bills.

All these things can work only when are willing to do it and want to save your money.

My grandma always used to scold for spending money on useless things and asks to save every penny for tomorrow because she has faced a lot of problems in her life economically, when she was just 16 year old her father passed away and left her alone with responsibility of younger 2 sisters, 2 brothers and mother. Because of no elder family member was there to take responsibility of family she had to

go to earn money and left her education for that.

She was so studious and intelligent among her classmates. She started doing farming in fields day and night with her mother, this is how she managed to earn money and give education to her younger siblings. She always wanted to be educated and make feel proud of herself, but it could not happen because of responsibilities. She will always that one regret in life of not being education just because of economic conditions and that's why she knows the value of each penny.

It's better to get serious about our savings and wise on spending money than to regret tomorrow.

III

BANK ON IN RELATIONSHIPS

Relationships are of different kinds and names, but all they have a base of trust whether it is a family relationship, friendship relationship or a romantic relationship.

Some relationships you get since take birth in this world like family and some are what you choose to make like friends and partner.

Relationships are like flowers, they need time, love and care. If no, then they will start losing its freshness, fragrance, beauty and soon can shrivel.

Everyone needs a relationship and they make at least one after coming to this world.

We people always needs a person who could understand us, listen us and care for us. But why we can't be that person of someone, don't keep expectations in relationships it could destroy you from inside. Always be a person who offers nor expects from others, always try to understand each other.

IV
Family

In a family we finds people of different mentalities, age groups, religious outlook etc. Having a family is a great victory in itself because you have people to multiple your happiness and decrease your pain. You will never feel lonely because of them. Because of so many fights we will be still together.

It's a say that "the family who eats together stays together", spend at least some time with your family to avoid distance in relationships. It's ok to have problems and fights between family members because it's normal but it's not to let that destroy your relationship.

Unconditional love that you get from your family members is totally precious, having a family is cannot be defined as important or not because its everything in life. Distance cannot eradicate one's love for his family, from the beginning till the end we will find our family always be with us, others things may leave.

It doesn't matter how much bigger your house is , what really is love in between its family members. A house without a family is just a monument of bricks, cements and pillars. The people who stays there and make each moment precious is called family.

Don't count mistakes of your family, just focus on good vibes that you get from your family, whenever you need them they are with you even if they don't want to do so, it's a connection, love and concern they have for you.

Problems you would face in family but you should keep in mind you want to remove problems from life not family from life, have patience and go through with difficulties like-

Financial problems are very common and arduous to deal with. By minimizing your expenses and doing any small job you can help your family.

Medical emergencies are far similar to financial, sometimes situation comes you are ready and can't even decide next move like accidents, flu, any disease or disability. With each other's support and love these situations can also be face.

Education is one of serious and common problem of a backward family, who deals with many people who just want to take benefit of their illiteracy and gain money as much as they can.

It's very important for coming generation to take education and protect their family from these things.

Sometimes children of family takes wrong path and start practicing bad habits, it's a very delegate situation to handle by family members. The family members should exhort children fluently and have patience that they will understand.

V
Friendship

Friendship is something which is free from worries, hatred, sorrows and distance. It comes on relationships that you choose and you are the only one who can decide how you should redeem your part in it, there is no kind of pressure and compulsion.

Friends are as important as family members, they know you , loves you support you, believe you and never want you to feel lonely. With them you can share anything and anytime because they are the only one who can understand your situation, your worth and your feelings because of same age.

With your friends you are a person you want to be,

there is no formality or any kind of discomfort. Friends give you space to cherish in your own good deeds by hand in hand. To have a true friend now a days is very rare and lucky in itself, it's a say that quality matters but quantity don't ; it's ok to have few friends in life but it is not ok to have so many of no worth, selfish mindsets, negative vibes etc.

Everyone knows what a true friend is but sometimes we get blind because of temporary things or materialistic things like high economic possessions, outer appearance, fake conversations and any other reason. It's better to choose good friends on time to have a happy life and not to fool yourself.

The world famous friendship of Krishna and Sudama shows us the value of it in every aspect.

Whenever someone wants to give a true example of friendship than they call Krishna and Sudama.

I want to share this mesmerizing and heart touching story with you , many years ago there was an aasharam(where students take their education) where Krishna and Sudama were students and take education from same Guruji . They were very good friends and have a strong bond between them.

They used to look after each others happiness and care needs. As the time passed they went to their natives and soon Krishna become the king of Dwarika and enjoys all wealth and luxury but on other hand Sudama was facing so many difficulties in his life such as poverty, family responsibilities, proper facilities etc.

One day Sudama's wife asked him that you often so many talks about your friend Krishna king of Dwarika why don't you go to Dwarika and ask for help from Krishna . Sudama was bit dither about going there because now he is not just his friend he is a king and have a strong possession.

He was confused that what he should take to give him, Krishna have everything and he also could not afford big and expensive gifts to offer Krishna as he is going Dwarika for the first time when he became king.

Then, Sudama's wife bring some rice from neighbour's and asked Sudama to take this along with you to give Krishna.

Sudama started his journey with a hope of meeting his friend

and at the same hesitation of meeting a king. Sudama when reached palace of Krishna the guards standing ask him who are you and what you want, he replied call Krishna tell him that his friend Sudama come to meet him, one of them go and call Krishna, the moment Krishna heard that his friend came to meet him he got exited, happy and began to run towards Sudama.

He take him inside the palace and started doing hospitality by washing his foots with milk, arranging a table with different dishes etc. Everyone was surprised to see the king doing these things for his friend who is just a simple man not any big personality.

Krishna asked Sudama what you brought for me

show but Sudama was bit hesitate to give him then Krishna himself take pouch of rice from him and start eating very happily.

He could not tell Krishna about problems he is facing and planned to go his town soon. After staying few days in palace of Krishna, he returned to his cottage when he reached his cottage, he got shocked and start wandering because there was a huge, beautiful and mesmerizing palace in place of his cottage. He understood it was only Krishna who did this for him even without asking and saying a single word about his condition.

This way a true friend get to know about his friends problems without saying.

VI
LOVESHIP

Trust is basic fundamental need of any relationship. For a healthy and life long relationship partners need to be have trust in each other. Their should be no confusion or doubt after being in relationship, it's ok to clear all doubts and confusion before getting into it because it's a say that ,

"before getting into relationship open your eyes fully but once you get into relationship close half your eyes."

There should be no insecurities between you and your partner because it will not let you to live as you want and it could be distressing for your partner also. A person needs to have someone who

always listens all his talks, to give moral support and advice without getting judge whenever there is need that's why he/she get into a relationship.

Everyone needs to understand this even though you are in relationship with someone still individuality of both the person will never fade. The freedom that you both give to each other in taking decisions for ones sake will make your relationship stronger and provide that space that anyone could desire for.

We usually forget this and start interfering between each other's decisions and personal space. We have no rights to stop someone from taking their decisions and controlling their life even they are

our life partners. It's our responsibility
to give love and respect what our partner deserves.

Loving a person is need of relationship but with loving you need to be respectful with your partner because it's not a choice but duty.

Having respect for person even if you don't love them shows how well your parents raised you and have given you good qualities to live your life. Because wherever you go whatever you do you are the representative of your parents.

" Sometimes a person can make you feel in 10 days what a person can't make you feel in 10 years".

You will realise when you see or meet that person who is made for you.

God will send signs to you so that you can understand that he/ she is the one.

It's just that believe in God and trust
your intuitions, they never lie to you.

It's a

say that do if you are willing to otherwise don't . If you don't want to be with that person with whom you are now but still continues for the sake of people and their feelings than don't be with him/ her because ultimately you are not happy and your happiness is all what matters.

Stay because you want to stay, leave because you want to leave. You can't keep others happy by fooling yourself because end of the day you lost yourself. The real happiness of having someone is with having you yourself as well.

VII
RESPECT DIFFERENCES

We people see a lot of different styles, peoples, languages, houses, trees, colours, traditions, customs, etc; in our daily life. Some are rich whereas some are poor, tall or short, fair or dark, fat or skinny. It's an element of nature that no one is same or inferior than any other thing or living being, everyone and everything is unique and have its own definition to this world.

God has made for some specific reason
that we will know one day.

Almighty expects from us brotherhood and respect among eachother.

We people don't realise the value of things or people until they leave us or disappear. Before time will teach us the lesson of giving importance to everyone and

everything what we have, we should learn it now. No one will remember which colour dress you wored, whether your nails were painted, your hairstyle, your makeup, etc but one thing they will definitely remember is how you treated them.

A person is define by his/her behaviour or attitude, people love to talk with the person who behave well and there should be no place of humiliation.

Once there was a Rich man who was arrogant, self centered, egoistic and usually don't talk to people who are not well equipped or economically strong. He used to insult workers of his apartments and workplace, sometimes because of their attire or language, other times for their illiteracy.

The reason keeps changing but his behaviour didn't. It was in a habit of that rich man to insult people of poor families.

One day, the rich man was discussing with her wife that he will have an important meeting tomorrow and anyhow he have to reach on time for which he have to get up early in the morning and catch his flight. This meeting was not as usual like other meetings he had before, this opportunity could prove to a lifetime opportunity to him for which he was exited too.

Next day, he was ready to go with his all belonging and preparations.

The same day, worker of his building who used to collect garbage from every house and dump in the

dumping ground enter in the building for his daily routine.

His name was Vivek and was famous in that area because of his hard work and honesty. He started going and collecting waste materials from every house of each floor. He was using the lift which is available only for the people of society and their relatives not for the workers who work there.

Vivek had no other option because the lift was not working and he was getting late for his work. As he reached infront of the house of that rich man whose name was Samrat , he rings the bell an enraged voice come out that,

"its there only take that and get lost". Vivek felt insulted and decided to ignore and get back to his work than he went to

Vandana's house (one of society member) whom he takes as his elder sister and Vandana also respects and love Vivek as her younger brother. The bond between them was so pure and irrespective of religion, social status and all society taboos.

Vandana asked- 'Vivek you can use the lift which is for society members , afterall you are doing society work'.

Vivek replied- 'If you insists than ok'.

He left for his remaining work by taking all that stuff. As he entered the lift and press the button of ground floor, he heard someone was shouting to stop and wait for me. And that person was no other but Samrat , he entered the lift and asked Vivek to press the button for ground floor.

Samrat was full of anger and started

feeling uneasy cause he don't want

Vivek to be with him in lift. He started yelling him by saying,

'You people have no class, smelling like garbage, look at your ugly face etc; tell me who allowed you to use this property'.

After a while suddenly electricity gone off and lift got stuck between two floors with two people in it. Samrat gets panicking as he was thirsty and have to catch a flight on time as well. Despite of rigorous behaviour of Samrat, Vivek still offer him a bottle of water and treat him nicely but Samrat failed to accept with anger. After half an hour people helped them to come out, as they got saved from that situation, Samrat started shouting to Vivek

' this was all because you have no idea I lost my deal worth of

lakhs. Do you even know lakhs consist how many no. of zeros, you people are useless'.

Then he replied with frustration- 'What you think we people have no work, no class, no value? If you think like that than let me tell you we people do have importance and our work is equally important as your work.

Without us you people can do nothing'.

The

whole society were standing and witnessing their fight there and try to stop them. Samrat start provoking everyone that this man should not come to this society and the sad part is this that many supported him and insults Vivek.

In between all this Vandana raised a voice that every work is valuable and worker too. He was just doing his job and he had done nothing wrong that he should get punishment or get fired from his job. But she could not be able to do anything for her and the whole scenario has become outrageous to Vivek that how his hardwork and honesty have no value in eyes of these people. He himself decided to quit his job and not to continue his visit in society.

Next morning as usual put their garbage infront of their house so that Vivek can take it but the passed garbage was still there, like this 3 days passsed and it was getting tough for people to manage all their household waste. Secretary of society called a meeting regarding condition of society cleanliness in which conclusion was that if Samrat will apologize to Vivek than only he will

come to his job again. Samrat refuse to say sorry and apologize to Vivek.

After a week Vivek come to society for his some work there Samrat was also standing ad talking to someone. Both saw each other and react nothing, after a while Samrat headed to Vivek and gave a taunt –

You again! Oh you may be need money wait i will give. This way he started insulting him again but suddenly he felt a stroke in his heart and fell down on the floor.

Vivek with his all presence of mind took initial steps and took him to his house. His family members thanked him for his work.

This time Samrat also understood that Vivek is a very humble, modest and good human being. He knewed that it's not make a difference whatever work

you do, it should be for welfare of human kind and legally right.

Also, no work is small or big, every work is important. Because it's a kind of worship to God, by doing our jobs we are greeting to God. Never discourage someone regarding his job or income. There are many people who do jobs according to their will and our happy. It's you how much capability you have according to which your income will.

VIII
VALUE YOURSELF

You are one of a kind in whole world. You don't need people's consent whether you are beautiful ,valuable, good enough to be with. It's you who decide I am important, I am a star of my own life. I don't need people to define me.

My cousin while doing her graduation met a girl who later on became a very good friend of her. She used to be very conscious about her looks, dress, makeup, perfume, whether her nails are painted or not rather to focus on qualities she already have. She always used to feel pity for herself as she thinks definition of beauty is fair colour,

certain height, size and glamour. In which she is totally wrong.

She started comparing her self with others including my sister and feeling insecure. One day there was a function in college and her roommates were getting ready for it meanwhile she also starts getting ready and trying new things that are totally different and extraordinary from her regular looks. After she finished her makeup, she was in this dilemma that doing extra and multiple layers of makeup can make her look good even if she don't need to be.

Her roommates didn't like the makeup she did because it was so strange and over but no one said a single word to her. No one wants to hurt her by saying anything to her. So

everyone decided to encourage her and take her along to party.

But my sister didn't want to lie with them and do false praise to her. She don't want that in party anyone make fun of her or say anything to her that she can't face or listen. So she decided to say her directly without any lie or false complements.

My sister: "Hey! If you don't mind can I

suggest you something about your look".

She said , "Yes you can, don't need to ask

just say whatever you want to".

My sister: "You are already beautiful , you don't need this extra makeup to hide your flaws or anything else. The makeup you wear right now don't look that much

good. So I prefer you should try something light and simple that can go with your skin tone easily.

She replied, "Look I know you care for me and you have no intentions to hurt me and I also know this that we cant comment or give our advice on someone's makeup or dress without that person's consent.

Now I will tell you why I wear this extra ordinary makeup as compare to everyday and did something more than casual because we people with dark skin and not that much good features try to look equal to you people who have fair skin, beautiful hair, charming body who don't need anything else to look good. By applying so many extra things and

makeup we just want to look at least not less than you people.

My sister: "I am so sorry I didn't know you have this much to think and manage for yourself. People says that unless you walk a mile on wearing someone's shoes, you don't realize the pain they are bearing.

Somewhere people do judge even saying repeatedly that they don't discriminate on basis of colour, creed or religion. It is visible clearly in their eyes and one can easily define the thoughts that person had for them. One thing we can really work with is ourselves. Just accept who you are no matter skinny, chubby, dark skin, fair skin and tall or short.

Because no one is perfect, everyone have flaws so just accept that, work on your sills and live life to the fullest.

Why we need others consent to feel good or look good?

Other people will always say something whatever you do or whoever you are so let them say. If you are satisfy with yourself wherever you are and whatever you do than ask yourself that whether it really affects me what they thin about me? No! so just be happy and enjoy your every single day on this planet. God will keep surprising you with good things and good people.

Let others keep judging you and commenting what they think of you but you should keep focusing on yourself and

ignore all the negativity you see around yourself. Remember you are the protagonist of your life and no one can live your life better than you.

IX
Things you should remember for life

There are battles you have to fight alone. There will be no other person standing with you for your whole life to support and show you the correct path.

You are unique and important, no other person can decrease your importance by their thoughts or behaviour to you.

Family comes first whenever you have problems. Respect and give love to your family.

This life is beautiful don't waste it by thinking too much. Just spend each day with learning new things

and pushing yourself to be good from yesterday

Be good to other people for no reason.

Everyone have problems don't get panic have patience and faith in yourself. Solve your problems with ground stage and try to solve step by step.

Be a person that everyone admires or loved to see. Qualities of a person defines them not how they look. Believe in good not bad, believe in giving not expecting.